To Lucy P—
who made the magic happen
EC

For Natalka, with love
LC

Text copyright © 2022 by Emma Carroll
Illustrations copyright © 2022 by Lauren Child
Photographs reproduced with permission from
The Frances Frith Collection and Alamy

First US edition 2023
First published by Simon & Schuster UK Ltd. (UK) 2022

Library of Congress Catalog Card Number 2022923517
ISBN 978-1-5362-3335-3

23 24 25 26 27 28 CCP 10 9 8 7 6 5 4 3 2 1

Printed in Shenzhen, Guangdong, China

This book was typeset in Wile Roman Pro.
The illustrations were done in mixed media.

Candlewick Press
99 Dover Street
Somerville, Massachusetts 02144

www.candlewick.com

MIX
Paper | Supporting
responsible forestry
FSC
www.fsc.org   FSC® C008047

The Little Match Girl STRIKES BACK

EMMA CARROLL

illuminated by LAUREN CHILD

CANDLEWICK PRESS

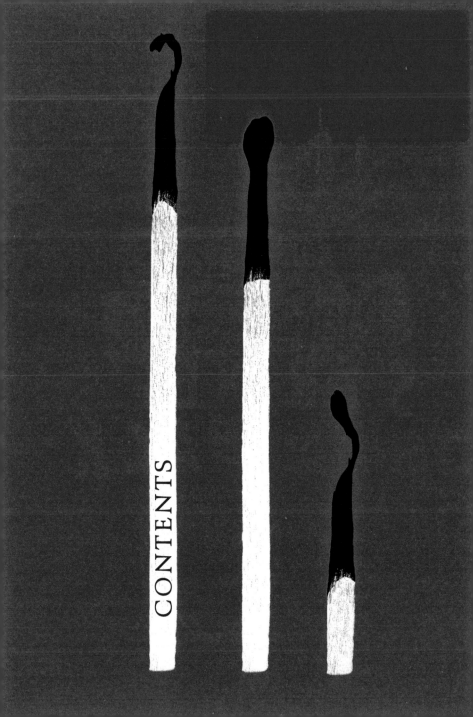

CONTENTS

one

THE
BORROWED
SLIPPERS

ONCE UPON A SNOWY NEW YEAR'S Eve, a story began. It was called *The Little Match Girl* and was sold, beautifully bound between chestnut-hard covers, at bookshops across the land. The story itself was so sweet and sad, people would snivel into their hankies upon reading it, and soon it became famous the world over. It made the man who wrote it very rich indeed, though I don't suppose he'd ever met a real match girl in his life. If he had, he'd have known we weren't all pretty things with fair curls and tiny, freezing hands, and that most of us were fed up with being hungry all the time. We didn't want people feeling sorry for us; we wanted a fair chance at a decent life, and to one day be able to tell our own stories, from our own mouths. This author hadn't done his research, not properly. If he'd bothered to talk to one of us, he'd know that even little match girls have names.

My mam had called me Bridie, short for Brigid, the only Irish patron saint who was a woman, and a brave, bold one at that. It was also my grandmother's name. She'd died back in Ireland, so I never met her, but I had red hair just like hers, Mam told me. And the same bony knees and gruff laugh, and a way of stringing words together that made people stop and listen, which helped when it came to selling matches. I had her surname, too: Sweeney.

So, that's me, Bridie Sweeney. I'm a match girl, just like in the world-famous story, though my version has a far better ending. But there's no need to rush on, when you have the rest of my tale to hear first.

I lived with my mother and little brother, Fergal, in a drafty room above a pawnshop in London's East End. The shop was in a tiny court, flanked on all sides by grime-streaked buildings in which other families, just like ours, lived and worked. All day and night, you'd hear fighting and crying and, sometimes, a bit of singing. When the sun shone, the space between the buildings was strung with laundry that never quite got dry. It amazed me to think that Queen Victoria herself lived in this same city, only a mile or so to the west. I bet *she* never wore damp underclothes or got nibbled by rats in the night. But that was London for you: home to the very richest and the very, very poorest.

Luckily, though our living space was small, there were only three of us to share it. My father was long gone—a deckhand on a visiting ship, so Mam told me, and a gentle soul who'd cried more than the

baby he'd left her with when he set sail back to Spain. We never saw him—or his tears— again.

As soon as I was old enough to yell "MatCHES!" I was put out on the streets to sell them. Near the docks, where we lived, the competition was fierce. Us street sellers outnumbered the rats, which was no mean feat. Thankfully, I learned the business quickly, and if I do say so myself, I was soon one of the best match girls around.

"You could sell flames to a fireman, you could!" Mam would say with a laugh.

Part of me was proud to be good at what I did. But that didn't stop me from dreaming of bigger, better things. Top of the list was not being hungry all day, every day. A close second was for the match factory to pay their workers a proper wage.

For we were all in the match trade, Mam, Fergal, and me. My brother, at six years old, should've been in school. But, as had been the case when I was his age, paying the rent was our priority. And so Mam often kept Fergal out of school to work at making matchboxes. Hunger made us all fast learners. Once Fergal had collected the paste, wood, paper, and red Lucifers labels from the factory, he'd spread it all out on the kitchen table and not move from his seat for ten hours straight. On a good day he'd make one hundred matchboxes and earn just two measly pennies for his work.

What I never understood was that he *liked* going into the factory, despite it being as grim a place as you could find. But Fergal insisted he'd made a friend there—an older boy called Kip.

"He's got a very nice fat pet dog," Fergal told me, which, as he was smitten with all animals, would've made the world of difference to my brother.

All told, gluing matchboxes wasn't really hard work: that happened on the factory floor itself where women, like our mam, stood at benches for fourteen hours at a time and kept working until the poisons they dipped the matches into made their teeth fall out.

Selling matches on the city streets, I at least got some air, even if it was syrup-thick city air that made your chest tighten and your nose-pickings turn black. London's streets swarmed with barrow boys, crossing sweepers, beggars, bruisers, lords, do-gooders, ladies holding their skirts above the muck, each and every one of them needing candles to read by, a stove lit, a soothing puff on a pipe. You couldn't get anywhere in this life without a light, and for that light, you needed a match. Walking the cobbles, yelling, "Flames for a farthing!" I was certain people needed my matches as much as

I needed their coin. It wasn't just about a little box of wooden matches: I was selling them comfort, possibilities, hope.

"Mine are *magical* matches," I'd insist. "One strike and you'll be in a better place. I guarantee it!"

Like they had for my grandmother, the words tripped easily off my tongue. I'd spin stories of far-off lands where no one ever felt cold, of lights that never dimmed, of flames the color of rainbows.

"These matches, my friends, will transform your life!" I'd tell the passersby.

Many would shake their heads and walk on. Those with children in tow might slow down briefly before dragging their charges on. Plenty more would buy my matches. And some poor souls, hope sparking in their exhausted faces, clearly wanted to believe what I said: that these matches would change things for the better.

I wasn't daft enough to believe it myself, though. Not then.

∴

On this particular New Year's Eve where *my* story begins, it was daybreak and so cold we'd slept the night in our clothes. The only items I'd taken off were my black laced boots, which, for some reason, Fergal was now clomping around in.

"Hand 'em over, Jack Sprat," I said. His brush with the measles the previous year had left him smaller than the other boys in our court, and Mam and me doted on him all the more for it.

"Can't," he insisted, pale-faced and earnest. "Mr. Gladstone's gone under the floorboards. If he doesn't know I'm here, he'll never come out." Mr. Gladstone was Fergal's pet mouse, named after our prime minister because of his huge whiskers.

At the hearth, Mam was on her knees trying to coax last night's embers back to life. It would've been easier to light the fire with matches, but the only ones we had were all boxed up for selling.

"Let him keep the boots on, Bridie," Mam pleaded. "He's got school today, and it's snowy outside. You know how weak his chest is; we don't want him catching cold. See, look how nicely they fit now."

She'd stuffed newspaper down the backs of them. Never mind that giving him my boots meant *I'd* have to walk the streets barefoot. But what she said about Fergal's weak chest was true, and because of that and how gloomy he looked over his lost mouse, I softened. I'd outgrown the boots months ago, so the choice was chilblains or blisters.

"Mr. Gladstone'll be here somewhere, Sprat," I reassured him, because in truth you were never far from a rodent in London.

"But he isn't! He's lost!" wailed Fergal, tears brimming.

It was more likely our neighbor's killer cat had found him, but I didn't say so. Instead, I gave Fergal the last heel of bread to keep him from full-blown sobbing.

"We'll have us a nice hot supper tonight," I told him, hoping the promise of food might cheer him up.

"So we will," Mam agreed.

Though I wondered what she'd be able

to eat, since she had trouble with a toothache again, and that morning her jaw seemed worse than ever, all swelled up like a billiard ball.

Meanwhile, my bare feet, as knobbly as old potatoes, already felt cold. Yet the bonus of such bitter weather would be the need for heat and light. With any luck, I'd sell my matches five times over and make enough for a whole roast goose for supper.

Mam, of course, read me like the leaves at the bottom of a TEACUP.

She took off her felt slippers and handed them to me. "These'll keep the worst of the cold out, won't they?"

Her slippers were almost worn right through and at least three sizes too big, though I had to admit they were warmer than the floor. The problem was walking in them: the only way I could keep them on was to waddle like a duck. At least by the time I left, I'd made my sad little brother laugh, which was something.

CHAPTER

two

GOOSE

OUT IN THE STREET, THE NEW Year's Eve morning that greeted me was gray and bone-bitingly cold. All the way up the road, our local knocker-up, Neddy Jones, was tapping on windows crying, "Rise and shine!" in a voice shrill enough to wake the dead. Though it wasn't snowing currently, it had done so in the night: the sidewalks were covered in white, trampled-down ice, which made it feel like walking on polished marble. Mam's slippers certainly weren't helping matters.

"Morning, Neddy!" I said when I finally caught up with him.

"Morning, miss!" Neddy was always my first customer, no selling patter needed. He bought his usual box of Lucifers.

Carrying on up the street, I made a couple more sales, until I reached the dairy on the corner. Judging from the row of steaming milk buckets lined up against the wall, I'd timed it just right. The milk was about to be taken to Covent Garden for selling, and before they went, the milkmaids always stopped for a pipe break. Two hot, sweaty girls with the biggest forearms you ever saw were now emerging with the last of the buckets.

Standing this close to the dairy, I had to remember to breathe through my mouth. Not because of the milk, which Mam said they thinned out with water, but because of the stench wafting up the cellar steps. The dairy kept ten full-grown cows down there in the dark. If the buckets were steaming, I dreaded to think what that cellar floor was like.

"Need a little magic light in your lives, misses?" I asked, offering my tray of matches.

The tallest girl pretended to look serious. "Depends, don't it, Mags?"

"Too right," her friend agreed. "See, we're quite particular about the magic in our matches."

I enjoyed this type of playful banter.

"Today's matches are a rare treat," I promised the milkmaids. "Imagine yourselves somewhere calm and peaceful, like a forest or a riverbank—"

"Where it doesn't stink of cows," the tall girl interrupted.

Mags laughed. "Oh, go on, Rosie, you love your cows!"

"One strike of the match and your whole world will be transformed," I continued. "You'll hear birdsong, the river flowing, feel the sunshine warm on your face. All you have to do is stare into the flame."

It was pure fancy, of course. They'd heard

it all before, though I tried to say it differently each day: the river might become the seaside, or the birdsong a lovely feather bed. As for me, the only magic I was interested in that morning was the type that would conjure up a nice plump goose for our supper and a warm fire for un-numbing my toes.

.:•

After the dairy, I turned right, following the road until it widened and shops began to line the sidewalks. Thankfully, a path had been cleared through the snow, which made walking in Mam's slippers a bit easier.

"Flames for a farthing!" I cried, selling as I went.

The sidewalks were busy with house servants and footmen, their arms full of packages, baskets, and boxes as they darted in and out of the shops for their masters and mistresses. If they didn't have a hand free to buy matches, I'd sidle up to their waiting carriages, where the drivers sat hunched under their livery cloaks.

"You'll not find finer matches in the whole of London town," I told them. "I swear on my grandmother's life, they'll not let you down."

"Your grandmother died years ago, lassie,"

remarked one driver, who happened to know our mam.

"Her ghost, then," I retorted quickly. "Dead or alive, she's not a woman you'd want to mess with. She was the arm-wrestling champion of the whole of County Cork."

I'd made that last bit up, and the driver, guessing as much, laughed.

"Weren't you selling *magical* matches yesterday?" he asked.

"We only want the magic ones," his groom agreed. "Don't go fobbing off anything else on us."

The drivers gave in then and bought a box. I'd hoped they might buy more, but it was nice to stand for a moment near the warmth of their horses and imagine the homes to which these carriages would soon be returning. Homes full of hot food and roaring fires, and mothers sewing for the sheer *fun* of it, rather than to mend their one and only petticoat before the last candle burned down. I sighed to myself. Dwelling on life's unfairnesses didn't sell matches, did it?

Within an hour, I had more coins in my pocket than matchboxes in my tray. It was a great start. If I kept selling at this rate, we'd have the good supper I'd promised Mam and Fergal. Outside the butcher's, I cast a longing look at the geese, hanging up in rows by their limp necks. Just to think of one roasted, crispy and golden brown, made my mouth water. A few spuds, a carrot, all swimming in meat gravy, and Fergal's little face flushed with joy at the

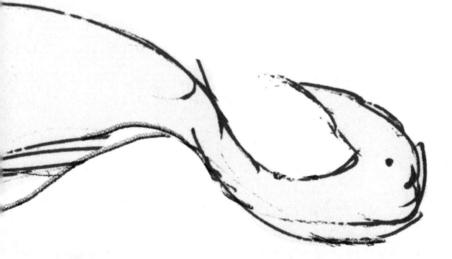

sight of his heaped plate—it was enough to give me the courage to ask a price. Street sellers like me were looked down on by proper shopkeepers like the butcher, and sure enough, he wasn't friendly.

"Don't you go touching nothing," he warned.

"I only want to ask how much."

"More than you can afford," he growled. "So clear off—you're scaring my customers."

I felt hot and uppity, ready to answer back. But a young fair-haired woman inspecting the pheasants then whispered to me, "They're one shilling per pound."

The butcher noticed.

"Really, Mrs. Besant, don't encourage her," he complained.

"*Really*, Mr. Clegg, we're all God's creatures," she replied coldly, then turned to me with a twinkle in her eye. "I'd try the butcher on Windmill Street if I were you. You'll get much better service."

I thanked her and left, trying to swallow my shock. A whole *shilling* for a pound of goose? Now, I was no scholar, but I knew I'd need more than the coins in my pocket to buy even the smallest, scrawniest bird for our supper.

From then on, I worked doubly hard to sell what matches remained in my tray. I told wild and wonderful stories of magical kingdoms and buried treasure, of galloping ghost horses on deserted beaches, of pirate princesses taking the high seas by storm. As the nearby church bells of Saint Mary's rang nine o'clock, I sold my last box of matches. I couldn't remember ever selling so much so fast. All told, I felt pretty satisfied, though I still hadn't made enough to buy the supper I had in mind. I needed more stock to sell.

And that meant going to the match factory.

CHAPTER
three

THE
FACTORY OF
NIGHTMARES

BUILT OF THE CLEANEST, REDDEST brick you'd ever find in this part of the city, the factory was hard to miss. It stood two stories taller than the surrounding houses and had the stern, stark look of a place people got sent to for punishment. A high wall surrounded the building, shielding most of the daily work from public view. Visitors were admitted through a set of intimidating iron gates. The workers had a smaller, shabbier entrance around the back.

Nearly two thousand women and girls worked at the match factory, my mam being one of them. Most of the workers lived in the streets and courts directly behind the factory building, but Mam said she'd rather walk half a mile home than live so close to the smell. The stench hit me the second I was in the yard. Phossy fumes, we called them—the bitter, chemical stink of the white phosphorus that made the matches burn.

Outside, the smell was off-putting enough; I couldn't imagine how bad it was inside the factory building. Mam was a dipper, dunking the matchsticks in the phosphorus, which meant she—and many others like her—

stood bent over the stuff all day long without so much as an open window for air. It was well known that these fumes were making the dippers sick. The bosses denied it, of course, saying it was drinking gin that made people's teeth go bad. Our mam insisted this was pure rubbish.

"I suppose they think this is gin, too, do they?" she scoffed, showing us her skirt hems one night.

In the dim candlelight, the fabric glowed with little specks of white. Some nights her fingers did, too, or the ends of her hair where she'd pushed it off her face. We'd thought it was brilliant, Fergal and me, calling it fairy dust

or star shine or whatever nonsense tripped off our tongues. But it stopped seeming so brilliant when Mam's teeth began to hurt.

As her tooth had seemed especially bad this morning, I decided to check that she was holding up. You see, there *were* windows in the factory—tall arched ones, which followed you like disapproving eyes—and though they were never opened, they gave a decent view of the factory floor. Reaching the nearest one, I stood on tiptoes, hands cupped to the glass.

Inside was a vast room full of workers, all standing in rows and in constant motion like a giant machine. Spotting Mam was near impossible. The women all looked the same: gray-faced, bone tired, and a fair few had swellings, just like hers, on their jaws.

Being a dipper was awful work, and it made me glad to be selling matches, not making them. The women were at their workbenches all day, even eating their bread-and-butter lunches there, though woe betide anyone who dropped crumbs. If their workbenches—or their hands, aprons, and feet—weren't spotless, they'd get a hefty fine from the factory foremen.

These foremen were bullies. The worst of a bad bunch was Mr. Scott, who had a soft, babyish face. He'd once fired a woman for fainting with hunger and was often seen on the streets over-whipping his poor horse.

Out of everyone on the factory floor, it was Mr. Scott I recognized. And just my luck that he'd noticed me, too, peering in at the window. He raised his fist and mouthed a silent threat. I ducked down quick, not wanting Mam to get into trouble, and hurried on to the factory storehouse.

⁙

"Sold out already, eh?" remarked Mr. Merriman, the stock controller, who, as the single most unsmiling person I'd ever met, didn't live up to his name.

"Sold every single box," I told him proudly. "I'll be back for more before the day's out."

Mr. Merriman looked unimpressed. "That's precisely what the other boy said."

"What other boy?" I asked, interested to know who else was doing a roaring trade today.

"Small chap. Wearing an old soldier's jacket."

"Is he new here?" I asked.

"New to selling, yes. Said he needed the extra money. Filling his pockets and his tray to the brim, he was. Says Roman Road market's heaving and he can hardly move for customers," he went on, clearly enjoying the fact that I was now scowling.

Roman Road market was my patch. I was heading there next.

"Ain't he the lucky one," I retorted, and filled my tray with matches and left.

•:•

I stormed out of the factory gates. At least I tried to; it was more of a frustrated waddle with Mam's slippers on my feet. But I was determined to find this boy and set him straight. It wasn't decent to cut in on another seller's turf.

The people knew me here; they expected my special patter, the promise of magic matches. He needed to get his own patch and keep out of mine—otherwise I'd never afford a goose.

It was snowing again. Already, the cleared sidewalks were disappearing under a fresh layer of white. The route took me over the railway line and past the asylum. Though the roads were still jammed with carts and carriages, everything sounded quieter, as if I'd shoved my head under a blanket. In the distance, the river Lea shimmered darkly as it wound its way down to Limehouse, where it met the mighty Thames. Often I'd wonder

at the beauty of this city, and how it existed side by side with all the hunger and filth. Right now, I was too angry to think anything, other than what I'd do to that rascal of a boy when I found him.

As it was, I caught up with him almost *too* easily. I'd taken the shortcut through Newhouse Court, which was such a grim, dark, rat-infested place, even I'd usually think twice about coming this way.

In the middle of the courtyard, his feet straddling the gutter, was my rival. It had to be him because, just as Mr. Merriman had said, he was wearing an old blue soldier's jacket with red embroidery and brass buttons, the pockets bulging with stock. He was selling matches to a woman with a bawling baby on her hip.

"Oi!" I called out, my voice booming off the walls. "I want a word with you, match boy!"

The boy spun around, eyes flaring wide. I knew a guilty face when I saw one—and from the speed with which he shot off across the yard, he had a guilty pair of heels, too.

"Come back here!" I cried.

He didn't stop. What's more, he knew the way out, diving behind the half-rotted door hiding a narrow alley that led out directly onto Roman Road. Bunching up my tatty skirts,

I went after him. I barged through the door just in time to see him shooting out the other end of the alley.

"Wait!" I yelled, tearing after him. "You little pest, *wait!*"

I emerged from the alley, blinking at the bright snow. The traffic on Roman Road was moving quickly. On the other side of the street, where the market stood, I caught flashes of the boy's blue coat with red embroidery as he flitted between the stalls. I was in danger of losing him. In a gap in the traffic, I darted across the road.

What happened next happened fast.

A
whoosh
of wheels
on slush.
Horses **snorting**,
the smell of leather.
Someone shouting.
A woman's scream.
Me FREEZING in my tracks
as the force of a passing carriage,
JUST A HAIR'S BREADTH FROM MY FACE,
knocked me off my feet.

CHAPTER
four

THE
SLIPPER
STEALER

THE CARRIAGE SAILED BY IN a blur of gleaming black horses and rust-red paintwork. I landed hard on my backside in the middle of the street. My matchboxes, scattered far and wide around me, were now crushed underfoot or sinking soggily into the slush. Grabbing what I could save, I tried not to cry. Every one of my bones hurt. And when I saw my tray, smashed to bits in the gutter, the shock made me giddy. I was lucky to be in one piece.

As the carriage disappeared around a corner, wheels spraying unsuspecting pedestrians with slush, I suddenly realized: the carriage belonged to Mr. Bryant, the match factory's owner. It felt like a punch to the stomach, and I fought down furious tears. Here I was, selling Mr. Bryant's wares, and he couldn't even slow down to let me cross the street!

"Brute!" I yelled in the direction he'd gone.

More carriages were swerving around me as if I were a stone in a river, with shouts of "Move on, love!" and "Fancy stopping there!" while no one offered any help. I wondered miserably if the soldier-jacket boy was nearby, having a good gloat.

Scrambling up, I made it to the curb, where I saw, to my dismay, that I was no longer wearing Mam's slippers. They must've come off when I fell.

"Double drat it!" I cursed.

In the frenzy of carriage wheels and hooves and churned-up ice, there was no sign of the slippers. I knew they weren't worth stealing. More likely, they'd gotten caught in a wheel or pounded to pulp under a horse. The tears I'd been holding back spilled down my face. Mam had lent me those slippers in good faith. And I'd lost them. I'd lost my matches, too, and half my customers, thanks to some little pest thieving my patch. Everything that could go wrong had. With my arm flung over my face, I sobbed angrily into the crook of it.

Why was life *so* unfair?

Yet, despite my wretchedness, something of my grandmother's spirit flared up in me. I still had coins in my pockets. And, once I stopped blubbing, I realized I had a few matches left to sell. I also had a score to settle with my rival. Perhaps I should tell him that my grandmother was the arm-wrestling champion of County Cork and see how he liked it.

Walking without Mam's slippers was easier at first.

"You haven't seen a boy—blue coat, dark hair?" I asked the market sellers as I wound my way between the stalls.

No one had. The market crowds were thinning, and many of the stallholders had begun to pack away early, muttering about how bitter cold it was and wanting to get home in time to celebrate the New Year.

In truth, I had no idea where the boy would go or whether he knew all of the area as well as he'd appeared to know Newhouse Court. The best thing was to keep moving, and keep selling as I went. It helped to think of something other than the burning cold in my feet.

"M*aaa*tches!" I cried, shivering. "Come and buy your

m – m – m – m – magic

m – m – m – m – m – matches!"

Though after their tumble in the street, my matches looked far from magical. What boxes I'd managed to save were damp, their labels peeling off. When I did sell a box, the man quickly threw it back at me after the matches failed to light his pipe.

"*Magic?* Blooming rubbish, more like!" he snorted.

The damp boxes being the problem, I

got rid of them and began to sell the matches on their own.

"Special-edition matches! Once-in-a-lifetime chance!" I told people. "These Lucifers are so good, ladies and gents, I'm selling them one at a time!"

I bet even the soldier-jacket boy couldn't think on his feet so fast. But I was beginning to suspect that he'd sold all his stock and gone home. There was no sign of him, and no one wanted to buy my matches, despite my best efforts. As well as the cold numbing my feet, I was hungry, too. All the tricks that took your mind off an empty belly—chewing a fingernail, gulping down fresh air, singing a song—weren't working. That dinner I'd promised Fergal seemed more important than ever. A goose might be stretching it, I was beginning to admit, but I wasn't going to go home empty-handed.

Before I knew it, I was walking up Windmill Street. It was a busy little road lined with silk workers' cottages and shops selling everything from false teeth to rat poison. Remembering what the nice lady had said about the butcher here being cheaper, I paused outside to see what my pennies would buy. The butcher himself was wiping down rows of empty meat hooks. I got the feeling I was already too late: the whole shop looked picked clean.

"A goose? Nah, sorry, miss. They all went hours ago." The butcher shook his head. "And I've just sold my last chicken to him."

He pointed to someone behind me; I turned to see who. When I realized it was the soldier-jacket boy, he was already running. To my utter amazement, he had Mam's slippers tucked under his arm.

"You louse-bag!" I cried. "Come back here and show me what you're made of!"

I tore after the boy. He was quicker than me, though, darting down alleyways I didn't know existed and leaping over walls like a champion steeplechaser. I didn't have the strength to keep running for long. The icy, gritty sidewalks made my feet sting. All too quickly, I'd lost him again. I shook my head in disbelief. First my customers, then my footwear. I'd been right to think he was up to no good. This boy wasn't a match seller—he was a low-down thief!

Meanwhile, the snow was falling faster, as thick as feathers from a split pillow. It'd gotten darker and colder, too, as if daylight were giving up on the world. Chasing after the boy wouldn't put food on the table. Heavy-hearted, I started walking again toward the smell of coal fires in the hope of selling my last few matches.

Within a street or two, the houses

became bigger and finer. Tomlin's Grove, Mornington Road, Merchant Street were lined with the sort of places that had servants who, from my experience, used matches aplenty. You could see as much in their lovely lamp-lit windows, twinkling Christmas trees, and crackling, flaming hearths. From outside on the frozen sidewalk, these cozy homes looked like slices of heaven. It made me wonder what work the people did who lived here, because it didn't seem humanly possible for anyone to work harder than those at the match factory. Yet the twenty-five shillings a week Mam earned barely covered the rent of our tiny room.

Rumor had it that Mr. Bryant's house was bigger still, with front steps and a footman who answered the door. There'd be a stable around the back for his glossy horses and for sheltering that lethal rust-red carriage. It didn't seem right that some people should have so much and some of us so little.

Up and down each street, I knocked on back doors, basement doors, doors that opened directly onto hot, busy kitchens, where smells of roasting meat made me hungrier than ever. The cold had gotten to me, making me shiver so hard my hands were shaking. Some maids shooed me away; the ones who didn't picked over what I had to offer, leaving the dampest matches.

By the time I'd reached the last street, the coins in my pocket didn't feel any heavier. At the very last house in the row, I knocked doubly hard.

"Are you needing matches, missus? Special, magic ones that make your wishes come true?" I offered as the door opened.

A young, well-dressed woman stood in a pool of light. She didn't look in need of wishes, frankly.

"No, thank you, I . . ." The woman bit her lip, frowned. "I say, I know you, don't I?"

"I d-d . . . d-d . . . d-don't think so," I stuttered in surprise.

But she seemed sure of it. "Yes, I remember. It was the butcher's, wasn't it? You wanted to buy one of those dreadfully overpriced geese?"

If it was the same woman, then she looked totally different hatless, with her soft, light hair unpinned. I really wasn't certain it *was* her, and after the day I'd had, I was suspicious. Anyone who worked the London streets had heard stories of child snatchers. They'd buy you soup or give you a blanket, claiming to be long-lost family or a charity worker, then before you knew it you'd be in chains, laboring down a mine or up a chimney.

Yet the truth was I was *that* cold and *that* hungry, if the woman did offer soup and blankets, I didn't trust myself to refuse. It was safer to turn my back and limp away.

CHAPTER
five

THREE
BROKEN
MATCHES

AT THE END OF THE STREET, I stopped in an alleyway to count the day's earnings. I wasn't expecting much after losing most of my stock on Roman Road. The amount was truly dismal. All that walking, all that selling, all that talking and storytelling, and I'd still only made enough for a couple of small meat pies. I slumped against the wall. There was no flaring of my grandmother's spirit this time, no spurring-on from my long-dead namesake. I felt miserable to my core, and too hungry to think straight.

Mixed in with the coins, deep in my pocket, were three remaining matches. They were so crooked and damp, no one was going to buy them. It was tempting to hurl them into the gutter—and stamp on them for good measure—but I couldn't summon the energy even for that. Instead, I found myself picking out one of the matches and striking it against the brickwork.

It crackled,

and spluttered

into

fizzed, uncertain

life.

"Stare

into

the

magic

flame,

and

you'll

find

all

you

could

wish

for ..."

How many times had I trotted out that line to customers? It was ridiculous to think people fell for it. A match was a cheap wooden splint dipped in nasty poison, which made factory owners rich and their workers sick.

Where was the magic in that?

Yet for all my banter, I'd never really looked into a flame before, not properly. This one was shaped like a petal or the head of a spear. At the bottom, it glowed blue, then white, then burst into the brightest sunset orange. What little heat the flame gave off felt delicious against my icy fingers. All too quickly, it reached the end of the match.

And this was the strange part: though the

match had burned to black, the flame hadn't gone out. If anything, the warmth of it grew, spreading along my arms and across my face. I kept gazing into the flame.

What would I wish for? I wondered. That was easy: I'd wish for a different life where I was rich, with fine friends who lived in a huge house and who'd invite me to supper parties every week.

My head swirled with pies and custards, roaring fires and warm woolen dresses, and the sheer joy, just for a moment, of forgetting how cold and hungry I was. It was then that I saw a shape in the flame. I blinked, supposing I'd imagined it. Until it came again, moving from left to right across the light.

This time I studied it so closely, I almost went cross-eyed from looking. And even then I could hardly believe it.

The shape was, in fact, a tiny carriage pulled by miniature horses, trotting across the whitest part of the flame. I'd never seen anything like it, not even in the window of London's fanciest toy shop, where you could buy miniature soldiers and cart horses and ballerinas all painted to perfection. This carriage wasn't quite solid, the horses' hooves didn't touch the ground, and the whole scene seemed to shimmer.

All of a sudden, a whooshing sensation hit me. My insides flew upward, as if I were jumping off a high step. A moment of dizziness. The wall behind me wasn't there anymore. I was falling. Feet over head over feet.

The falling stopped with a jolt.

I found myself standing upright on a sidewalk I didn't recognize. The tiny carriage—life-size now—was disappearing down the street, and it seemed to have just dropped me off. All around me were huge houses with driveways and big bay windows and separate entrances for guests and servants. These were very fine residences—finer, even, than the homes I'd called on earlier when trying to sell my matches. I had no idea what I was doing here.

But I felt so warm, so comfortable, I supposed I was dreaming.

All too well I knew the dangers of falling asleep on a dark, wintry street: if the cold didn't finish me off, then thugs and pickpockets would. It was dangerous to stay here, in this dream. I needed to wake up.

Rubbing my eyes, I noticed I was wearing proper kidskin gloves! The leather smell, the soft creaking of my fingers, felt completely real. So did the sidewalk beneath my warm, booted feet and the swish of silk skirts against my ankles as I crossed the street. If this was a dream, it was the clearest, sharpest one I'd ever had. No amount of eye rubbing seemed to wake me from it.

At the first house I came to, I opened the gate and skipped up the front steps as if I'd been there many times before. The huge door was answered by a footman in livery.

"I've been invited for supper," I told him.

"So you have, miss," he said with a bow. "Good evening to you."

Once I was inside, he took the velvet cloak—*a cloak!*—from my shoulders. Then he showed me upstairs to the drawing room. Halfway up the stairs, as we passed a mirror, I caught sight of my reflection. The girl staring back at me wore a blue silk dress, her hair framing her face in perfect ringlets. It took a moment to realize that girl was me. The shock made me catch my breath.

My wish had come true!

This was who I'd be if I'd been born into money. Mam, Fergal, and me, we'd live on a street like this and be invited to houses like these. Life would be a giddy whirl of parties and dresses; there'd be no more selling matches. No more being hungry. I could hardly imagine what that might feel like. Even in this dream world, my stomach still gave a hungry grumble.

In the drawing room, where lamps burned and a good fire roared, two plump, pretty girls my age sprang up from a sofa to greet me with sugary kisses. I had no idea who they were, but that didn't seem to matter—they knew me, all right.

Also in the room were a man and woman: their parents, I supposed. The woman beckoned me over to where she was sitting, on a chair pulled up close to the fire.

"It's wonderful of you to join us," she gushed, taking my hands.

Not sure what to say, I stared at the pearls at her throat, each one the size of a small turnip. The crackling fire felt hot through the thin fabric of my dress. I was aware of the father downing his glass of sherry in one swift gulp and muttering impatiently about having work to do after dinner, and could we please now get on with eating? My stomach rumbled again in reply. If the man heard it, he didn't say so, but one of the daughters did and laughed.

"Goodness! Someone's hungry!" she cried, as if I'd just grown a second head right there in front of her.

I clutched my stomach, embarrassed.

"Sorry," I muttered.

Aware now that being hungry wasn't the done thing, I tried not to seem too eager as the butler led us into the adjoining room. I'd expected a table groaning with food, but it was set simply with a cloud-white cloth, white plates, and silverware that sparkled.

I didn't want to seem rude, but I was terribly disappointed. Where was the roast goose, the pies, the fancy things in aspic? I'd hoped for meat, cake, jellies, and maybe, if we were really lucky, a sheep's head with the eyeballs still in their sockets, because those were the tastiest bit that everyone loved.

The two girls started bickering over where I was to sit and then sulked when their father said they were causing a scene. I was seated, eventually, close to the fireplace. The heat quickly grew stifling, yet what worried me more was the lack of food.

Then, thankfully, again
the butler appeared
with a huge tureen.
Clear beef soup was
ladled into our
dishes.

It
was
quite
tasty,
though
there
wasn't
enough
of
it.

I was glad when, after our plates were cleared, another course, of fish, arrived.

By now, I'd forgotten any attempt at politeness. My fish was all gone in a couple of mouthfuls, which then meant having to wait for the others, who took tiny bites from tiny forkfuls, then chewed for hours like well-bred horses. This was, I was learning, how fashionable people ate: instead of everything on the table at once, the food was brought in slowly, to be savored one delicious course at a time.

As for making polite mealtime chitchat, it seemed no one here expected girls to speak up or add anything sensible to the conversation.

Which was just as well because the food itself, and the different cutlery that went with it, took most of my concentration.

The meat course arrived next. After that came jellies, creams, trifles, and then another savory course, of pheasant, followed by cheeses and watercress, then a great platter of fruit. My dress had grown considerably tighter; the heat from the fire was making me sweat, too, but I kept eating. It was as if I was making up for every meal I'd missed in my life, in the hope that I'd never be hungry again. Even when I heard my dress seams creaking, I still held out my plate for more.

Nor could I quite believe that all this food

was for just the five of us. The girls and their mother had appetites of little mice, so most of it went back to the kitchens untouched. It shocked me to think of all that waste.

⁂

Once dinner was finished, there was much dabbing of dainty mouths and talk of retiring to the drawing room. I was so full, I felt ill. What I dearly wanted was fresh air, to get out of this stuffy, stifling room and take off my prison of a dress so I could breathe again. Remembering the wish I'd made into the match flame, I held my stomach and groaned. So much for rich food and fine company—I hadn't much enjoyed either.

When the footman announced that the carriage was ready to drive me home, I jumped to my feet so fast a button burst from my dress. It flew across the room, landing with a *ping* on the hearth, though, thankfully, the only one to notice was the footman, who didn't try very hard to hide his smirk.

Out in the street, a rust-red carriage was waiting, two gleaming horses snorting in their harness. I recognized the vehicle straightaway, and stopped dead.

"What's this?" I cried.

"It's your ride home, miss," the footman

explained. "In the master's carriage—aren't you honored?"

Honored wasn't the word for it; I was appalled. Despite the streetlamp's yellowy light, I recognized the carriage as belonging to Mr. Bryant, the match factory owner. It meant that the house where I'd spent the evening was also his, and the dull, thoughtless people I'd had dinner with were him, his wife, and his daughters

I'd been granted my wish of fine friends and fancy supper parties, but all this luxury, all these riches, were paid for by my mother's hard work.

Meanwhile, the footman was becoming impatient.

"Are you getting in the carriage or not?" he asked testily.

"Yes," I said, because I instinctively knew that there were rules to magic, and it was time for me to go home.

CHAPTER

six

MRS. BESANT
AND MY MAM

AT SOME POINT ON THE JOURNEY,
I must've fallen asleep, because when I
opened my eyes, I was back in the alleyway.
The velvet cloak I'd worn was once more my
gray, threadbare shawl. The gloves, the ringlets,
the fine dress—they'd all vanished, too. I was
cold to my very bones. And I was starving
hungry all over again.

Nothing else felt normal, though, now that I knew what my matches could do. Giddy with excitement, I felt in my pocket and found the last two. They were broken, with the phosphorus mostly rubbed away, and didn't look particularly magical. Perhaps it had all been a dream.

There was only one way to be sure. I chose the longest match, struck it against the brick wall, and it flared into life.

I studied it,
hardly daring to breathe,
making sure I'd be ready
if things took a peculiar turn.
But the flame burned too fast,
racing down the match toward
my fingers. The light was so
bright, it threw ugly
shadows across
the walls.

I tried

to keep my

hand still and

concentrate.

If I willed it,

if I believed in it,

then the magic

might begin.

"I wish that rich people like Mr. Bryant didn't have everything while poor families like mine have nothing," I whispered.

The match burned on.

Any moment now . . . Any moment . . .

I waited. Nothing happened. The flame hissed like any perfectly ordinary match about to die, which made me think I could've sold it, and so I grew more disheartened.

"Please, please, please!" I begged. "Give me my wish."

There was a flicker. A crackle. Then, just when I'd given up hoping, the whooshing sensation took hold. It was happening again! The magic sent me tumbling into blackness, head over heels, stomach in mouth. Thankfully, it lasted only a few seconds before I landed with a hearty thud on something soft and cushiony. An armchair.

For a moment, I sat there, stunned. As I gathered my wits, I saw that I was in what looked like someone's study. The room was warm, cluttered with books, a desk, more armchairs, and a tea tray laden with cake, which was being guarded helpfully by a gray-muzzled dog. This house, though very comfortable, wasn't in the same league as Mr. Bryant's. I liked it much more, and was starting to relax a bit when the door swung open. Two people—a young woman and an older man—came into the room. I froze in panic. Now I'd have to explain what I was doing in their house, and it wasn't as if I'd been invited this time.

What's more, I knew this woman. I'd tried selling her matches not an hour before, then run off when she was kind to me. Seeing her properly in the study lamplight, she was also, very definitely, the same nice lady I'd met at the butcher's. Child thief or not—and I was rapidly deciding she wasn't—she'd be alarmed to see me. She might even call the police.

I shuffled nervously in my chair, knowing I was about to be discovered. The woman took her seat at the desk. The man eased himself gingerly into the chair opposite mine and opened his evening paper. Bizarrely, neither of them seemed to hear or see me. They carried on as if I wasn't there at all.

"I'll continue writing letters to the news-paper until Mr. Bryant listens," the woman was saying. "Honestly, he's not kept his word on making any of the improvements we agreed on for the match factory."

"Indeed, you've not had much success with him, have you?" the man replied. "How long is it that you've been trying to make him listen?"

"A good while," the woman admitted. Then she added in earnest, "But I won't give up. These are people's livelihoods we're talking about. Workers are dying, children are losing their mothers and sisters, just to earn a pittance that doesn't even put enough food on the table."

The man looked up from his paper. "You've been to the factory, have you, Annie? You've seen this for yourself?"

"Not yet, though I've no reason not to believe what I've been told."

"Told by whom? The workers themselves?"

Annie looked indignant. "By Mrs. Hillingsworth at the charity."

"*Aha!*" The man tried not to smile. "The great Mrs. Hillingsworth! Living in a comfortable villa with four servants must make her quite the expert on factory work!"

I sat forward, eager to say something. But neither Annie nor her companion saw me move; I was as good as invisible.

Maybe I was invisible.

The magic must've worked differently this time. Yet doing a quick check of myself— pinching my arm, tugging my hair—told me that I was all here, all present and real. I'd trailed dirt in on the fancy rug, and left smut on the chair where I'd touched it. Now that I was thawing out, the stench of my unwashed clothes seemed stronger than ever.

"What's that smell?" Annie said suddenly, her nose twitching.

"Erm, that'd be me," I admitted.

At last, she looked straight at me.

"Gosh!" she gasped, hand on her chest. "It's you, the match girl! How did you get in here?"

If I had been invisible, I certainly wasn't anymore—at least not to her. The man, though, was reading his newspaper again, oblivious. This magic business was all very confusing.

"My name's Bridie, miss," I said, trying to stay calm.

I didn't know what was happening any more than she did, but a sense of purpose took hold of me.

"My mam will tell you what the factory's

really like." I stood up from the chair. "Will you come and meet her?"

⁙

This being magic, Annie didn't bring a coat or hat and no one noticed us leave. Though the night air was bitter, the quiet streets glittery with ice, neither of us shivered from the cold. The journey back beyond Roman Road and past the railway took mere moments. We arrived at the factory gates just as the women were walking out at the end of their shift. Against Annie's well-dressed, well-fed frame, it struck me how thin and gray the match workers looked. They plodded past us without a glance.

"Can they see us?" Annie asked.

"Only if we speak to them," I replied, because that was how it'd seemed to work between us.

At this point, I was starting to wonder where Mam was. The other women had gone, their weary goodbyes growing fainter as they disappeared down the street.

Something wasn't right. Mam was never the last to leave work. I decided to find out what was keeping my mother, and beckoned Annie to follow me through the side gate.

We heard the voices first, echoing off the

brick walls and rumbling around the factory yard. In a dark doorway, a lantern flickered. My stomach dropped, for the sickly yellow light shone on a very familiar babyish face.

"It's no good whining now, Mrs. Sweeney," Mr. Scott, the foreman, was saying. "I counted your bundles. You did less work than the others today—far less—and that's a problem to me."

"It won't happen again—I promise," Mam pleaded.

"Ah, but it will, because you're sick, and I can't have sick workers on the factory floor."

Mam, hugging her shawl over her bony chest, stared up at him. Oh, how I wanted, right then, to reach out and squeeze her hand. The swelling on her jaw looked bigger than ever; Annie, I noticed, couldn't take her eyes off it.

"Poor lady," she gasped. "It's the phosphorus that does it. Such a highly toxic substance, you know."

"Yes, I do know," I answered, a bit sharply. "Mam's been saying as much for ages. All the women have."

Annie shook her head. "It's so very wrong. There are alternative ways to make matches, but Mr. Bryant won't even entertain the idea of considering them. These women deserve so much better."

In the doorway, voices were rising.

"My family has to eat, Mr. Scott," Mam told him.

"This is a factory, not a charity," he replied coldly. "If you're not up to the job, go home, and don't come back tomorrow."

I couldn't believe what he was saying.

"He's giving my mother the sack!" I cried.

Annie gasped in horror. "That's appalling! She's sick because of the factory. They're responsible for this."

"Too right they are! That measly worm of a man!" I was about to barrel over and tell Mr. Scott to his face, but Annie pulled me back.

"Think, Bridie, think," she warned. "Appearing out of thin air and shouting won't help your mother."

"We've got to do something!"

"Well," Annie began, "I'm going to write another letter—"

"Letters won't feed my little brother!"

Annie blinked in surprise: I don't suppose she'd been shouted at much in her nice, happy life.

"All right, then," she said, slightly affronted. "What do you suggest?"

"Action. From the workers themselves. What if no one turned up for work in the morning? That would hit Mr. Bryant where it hurts."

"Yes, in his wallet," Annie agreed, warming to the idea. "You're absolutely right. If there are no workers, the factory can't function, and he'll lose money."

She seized my hands, suddenly excited.

"How do we do this, Bridie?" she asked. "Where do we start?"

I didn't get to answer. All of a sudden, the factory yard was blackening at the edges like a burning piece of paper. Mr. Scott's lantern grew dim. The magic was fading.

"What's happening?" Annie cried.

A blast of night air made me shiver, and I could smell the city streets, the coal fires and drains, sweating horses and baking pies. I heard doors slamming, the thump of snow-muffled footsteps. When I opened my eyes, I was in the alley again. I was cold, hungry, alone.

This time it was different, though, because we'd had an idea, Annie and me, of what might make a difference. And I felt the tiniest glimmer of hope.

CHAPTER

seven

THE
FINAL MATCH

THINGS GOT TRICKIER WHEN I tried to sit up. Above my left ear, my head throbbed; when I touched it, my hair felt sticky with blood. I groaned. I didn't need to check my pockets to know what had happened. I'd been robbed. The few measly coins I'd earned, the last crooked match—it was all gone. Frustration and exhaustion overwhelmed me, and I started to cry. I could just about bear losing the coins. But not the last match.

I *had* to have that final wish. I needed to know that life could get better for my family. Already, I'd seen that wealth like Mr. Bryant's wasn't all it seemed and that Annie was trying to stick up for workers' rights, even if she did have more to learn on the matter. Yet where did that leave Mam and Fergal? How would things turn out for us?

I sat up slowly, drowsily. The cold was making me so tired. If I didn't start moving right away, I'd never get up again. And in the morning, some poor devil would find me frozen to death, which wasn't how *this* match girl's story was meant to end.

On shaky legs, I walked along the alley.

I stopped at the point where it opened onto the street. Something made me look down at the sidewalk, at a spot where the snow was pitted with a frenzy of footprints. And there it was. My final match. As frail as a fingernail, it lay abandoned in the snow. The pickpockets hadn't wanted it and had thrown it aside.

Grinning through my tears, I picked up the match. It was, without doubt, a weedy-looking thing, split almost in two. It was also my last chance at magic. I took a steadying breath. "Do me proud, little match," I whispered.

It lit
right
away,
with
one
swipe
across
the
wall.

The
flame
rose up,
magnificent.

"I wish to see my family living a better life," I said firmly.

Cupping my hands around the flame, I watched and waited, trying to be patient. The visions came quickly, of a familiar bare staircase, a door that rasped when you opened it.

And then I was tumbling through the dark, falling and falling as if the ground didn't exist anymore and I'd be dropping down forever. The jolt, when it came, was sharp enough to snap a neck—though, luckily, not mine.

I'd landed on a patterned carpet I didn't recognize. There were boots on my feet. I wore a striped dress with a soft flannel petticoat underneath that fell to my ankles. Everything fit me and was clean, even my hair, which hung loose and lice-free around my shoulders.

The room I was in looked like home, only a much better version of it. The place felt warm, the fire burned hot, and the table was set with red-and-white china I'd never seen before. Yet I knew in my bones that this *was* my home, even the unfamiliar bits of it, and I was overwhelmed with gladness to be here.

In the center of our table sat a beautiful roasted goose, resplendent on a bed of crisp potatoes and parsnips. There were bowls of greens, sausages, a jug of meat gravy, and at the end of the table, on a fancy stand, a fruit jelly glinted like jewels in the firelight.

Taking their seats were Mam and Fergal. They, too, looked neat and respectable: Mam wearing a gray frock with a little brooch at her throat, Fergal in a shirt and waistcoat, his trouser-clad legs swinging eagerly as he held out his plate.

"What a feast!" I cried in utter delight.

Mam turned to me, smiling. "Come on, lovey, sit down before it goes cold."

Hungry as I was, I couldn't take my eyes off her face. Her jaw wasn't swollen, her eyes, sparkling, were no longer glazed over with pain. Seeing her so well was the most magnificent sight of all and filled me with great joy. We were a normal, happy family with food, warmth, and one another.

As I took my place at the table, though, the room grew dim. The happy feeling began to fade with it, because the magic was ending, and I was desperate not to leave when it was so warm here and the plate of food in front of me smelled so tantalizing. And what about the dessert? Couldn't I stay long enough just to try a bowlful?

"Eat up," Mam said, her voice sounding more distant.

I hunched over my plate, loading all the food I could onto my fork, but it was too late. Somewhere between the plate and my mouth, the food vanished. So did the warm room, and my family with it.

∴

All too quickly, I found myself back, sitting on the curb of the snowy street. The cold seeped into my skirts again, but instead of despair, I felt fresh determination. Now that I'd had my three wishes, I saw how they connected like links in a chain. Mr. Bryant's greed had led to Annie's letter-writing to the papers, and if the world actually listened, if conditions at the factory *did* improve, then Mam would get well again and we'd live a better life. It was the middle part of this chain, how we got the world's attention, on which everything hinged. We needed to do more than rely on educated people to write letters for us. The real fight had to come from the workers, because without us, there'd be no match factory at all.

I was about to get up from the curb when a figure appeared at the mouth of the alleyway.

"Bridie? Is that you?"

Though the streetlight was behind her, I recognized Annie's soft, well-schooled voice. She tucked her skirts against her legs to crouch next to me on the sidewalk.

"What a strange evening! I hardly know what happened, but we *did* visit the match factory, didn't we?" she asked.

I nodded.

"Incredible!" She shook her head, still dazed. "Will you come back inside, into the warm, so we can discuss it further?"

But I'd had enough of talking.

"You saw what it was like at the factory, how my poor mother was treated. We need to take direct action," I insisted.

Annie looked at me with what might have been admiration.

"What did you have in mind?"

"Something loud and public, and at the factory gates, so it'll get right up Mr. Bryant's nose."

Annie grinned. "A protest, do you mean?"

"Yes." I nodded eagerly. "That's it, exactly!"

⁘

By the time I finally got home, it was way past suppertime. My head was so full of magic and protests that I'd forgotten about my promise to bring back a goose. Now, seeing the bare table and cold hearth, guilt kicked me full in the gut. So did the sight of Mam leaping from her chair as I limped in through the door.

"Where have you been? I've been worried sick!" she cried. "Look at the state of you!"

She didn't look great herself. Her eyes were red-rimmed from crying. The swelling in her poor jaw was the size of an orange, and she was white-faced and shivering with cold. The room itself was bitter, frost glittering on the inside of the windows, a mean draft sneaking up through the floorboards. The only thing I was glad of was Fergal being asleep. It meant I didn't have to explain to him that I'd failed to bring home supper.

"I'm sorry, Mam," I said, feeling wretched. "I lost your slippers, and all my earnings, and my stock from the factory."

Some mothers might've gotten angry at that, but mine took my icy hands in hers and tried to rub some warmth into them.

"What happened, Bridie?" she asked.

"The selling was going well," I told her. "Till Mr. Bryant's carriage knocked me down and ruined my tray and my matches."

"Mr. *Bryant*? From the match factory?" Mam looked horrified. "So we've both lost our jobs today because of him, then?"

Broken, she slumped into the nearest chair.

"Oh, what shall we do?" she asked, fresh tears filling her eyes.

Now it was my turn to take her hands.

"We fight back."

Mam blinked. "Fight? *How?* I'm not tough like your grandmother, Bridie, so don't you be getting me into any scrapes."

"We don't have to do anything," I told Mam eagerly. "We simply stand our ground, that's all, and protest."

MRS.
GLADSTONE
ARRIVES

THE NEXT MORNING, I WOKE TO find Mam already up and dressed. Winter sunlight streamed in through the window. Dazed, I wondered how I'd managed to sleep through Neddy's knock-up call when usually he'd be tapping on the glass while it was still dark outside. We'd be late for work at this rate.

Then I remembered: Mam had been fired, and I'd lost all my stock. We didn't have work, thanks to Mr. Bryant. In my case, that pesky soldier-jacket boy hadn't helped matters, either.

Pushing back the blankets, I felt a strange mix of purpose and dread. We'd be hungrier than ever now without Mam's wages and mine. But yesterday had taught me that one decent meal wouldn't solve the problem. What we needed was better pay, better working conditions, and more fairness for the factory workers. We had a battle ahead of us—I knew that. But with our courage and Annie's connections and way with words, surely we'd make ourselves heard.

Fergal, meanwhile, had other worries.

"I still haven't found him," he said sadly when I joined him and Mam at the table.

It took me a moment to realize that he was talking about his missing pet mouse.

"You know what, Sprat?" I replied. "I bet Mr. Gladstone's gone on a wonderful mouse adventure—eating cheese, playing with his pals, standing up to cats."

It got a weak smile out of him at least and distracted him from asking what happened to last night's goose. To my surprise, there *was* food on the table—a couple of meat pies wrapped in gravy-stained paper, a twist of tea, a can of milk from the dairy up the road. The kettle was heating slowly over a small fire.

"Good thing we live above a pawnshop, isn't it?" Mam said, forcing a light tone.

On the mantelpiece was a space where our last brass candlestick had stood. It'd be dark here tonight, but the pies *were* delicious, though Mam didn't eat much. The pain in her jaw made everything difficult these days.

"You two dig in," she said, watching us fondly.

We ate quickly with our fingers, Fergal insisting on licking the paper. When we'd finished, Mam got up, crossed to the mirror, and put on her straw bonnet.

"I've decided. I'm going to the factory to ask for my job back," she announced.

My heart sank to the floor.

"Y-You can't!" I stuttered. Last night, I was sure I'd convinced her that we needed to act, that she shouldn't go back there until it was a safe place to work.

"I have to, lovey. Protests don't put food on the table," she said.

"But Mr. Scott can't treat you like that!" I cried. "You have to stand up to him."

She looked at me, exhausted. "And how do I do that?"

"Not on your own." I got up. "I'm coming with you."

As I grabbed my shawl from its peg, there was a sharp knock on the door. This was unusual: the only person to call was our landlord, and the rent wasn't due till the end of the week.

Warily, Mam opened the door. "Can I help you?"

In the gap between the doorframe and her shoulder, I caught a flash of red embroidery. Then the sleeve of a blue coat as an arm extended toward her. I stared in amazement. The soldier-jacket boy was on our doorstep!

Unable to hold back, I ducked under Mam's arm to face him myself.

"You've got nerve coming around here!" I cried.

He became flustered. "Oh! Um . . . I don't mean to—"

"You caused me enough trouble yesterday with your thieving and your trickery," I interrupted. "So if you know what's good for you, you'd better clear off!"

The boy took a step back.

"This person here," I explained to Mam, jabbing a finger in his direction, "stole my patch yesterday."

Mam tucked in her chin. "Did he, now? That doesn't seem right."

But Fergal, who'd heard the boy's voice, pushed past Mam's skirts, grinning in delight.

"Kip!" he cried.

"All right, Ferg?" On seeing a friendly face at last, the boy smiled.

"*Ferg?*" I glared at my brother. "No one calls you *Ferg!*"

Fergal shrugged. "Kip does."

I recognized the name. He was the boy with the very fat dog that Fergal knew from the factory. It all slotted into place now— why Kip was selling matches, how he knew where we lived. But I wasn't about to turn all friendly on him. In my book, he was still a sneaky thief.

Mam, though, had softened and, stepping back, invited Kip inside.

"Thank you, missus," answered Kip, as if he was politeness itself.

I remained unmoved. "You know, Mam, it was Kip who stole your slippers yesterday."

"I didn't steal 'em!" he cried. "I found them in the gutter."

"Huh! A likely story," I remarked. I'd searched the street for those blasted slippers, and they'd definitely already been taken.

"But it's true," Kip insisted, his eyes so wide and pleading I thought he was about to weep. "There'd been an accident earlier—a girl and a posh carriage, someone said—and afterward they'd had to sweep the road. The slippers were with a load of ruined matches and some broken wood—"

"Yeah, those were *my* matches and *my* tray," I muttered bitterly.

Still, he did seem to be telling the truth.

"I'm sorry." Kip then turned to Mam. "I didn't know they were your slippers, Mrs. Sweeney—honest I didn't. I only borrowed them. Here, you must have them back."

From his pocket he produced the left slipper. It looked so worn and shabby, it was hardly worth the effort, all told. But then, from inside his coat, he pulled out the matching right one. There was something inside it—I couldn't see what. This, he handed straight to Fergal.

"It's a bit bigger than a mouse, but I hope you like her," he said.

For a second I thought he'd brought us a rat. But the look of sheer delight on Fergal's face told me it was something far lovelier. Snuggled up inside the slipper was a little furry brown puppy. It woke up, yawned, then licked Fergal's gravy-covered finger.

My little brother's eyes were as big as two moons. "Is she one of Elsie's pups?"

Kip nodded.

"Elsie's your dog, right? The fat one?" I guessed.

Kip nodded again. "She had six in the litter. I've been working double hard to keep them all fed and warm."

"Looks like we've got another mouth to feed, then," Mam groaned. But, like me, she could see Fergal's joy, and it warmed her heart.

The pup was, without doubt, the sweetest, dearest thing any of us had seen in a long while.

"She's got long whiskers," I noticed. "What are you going to call her, Sprat?"

"Mrs. Gladstone," he decided.

For the first time since he'd lost his mouse, my brother looked genuinely happy again. Though it irked me to admit it, that little puppy was going to lift his spirits far more than a plate of roast goose. And now that I knew Kip had sold all his matches to keep his dog and her pups fed, suddenly he didn't seem such a bad sort.

CHAPTER

nine

STRIKING
BACK

WORD SPREAD LIKE WILDFIRE about Mam being fired. By the time we reached the factory, a crowd of women had already gathered at the gates. They welcomed us with a huge cheer.

"What's all this, then?" Mam asked, surprised and overwhelmed. "Shouldn't you be inside? The shift's about to start!"

"We heard what Mr. Scott did to you, Mary," said a gray-haired woman called Eliza. "It's a crying shame. We've got to take a stand."

"Absolutely," I agreed boldly. "I say it's time to go on strike, don't you?"

From the enthusiastic welcome they'd just given us, I was sure they'd agree.

But Eliza sucked in her cheeks. "If we strike, we won't be paid, and we've all got families to feed, though I can't see any other way to get Bryant's attention."

"You mustn't strike because of me!" Mam was horrified. "This is my business—I'll sort it."

"He won't listen to you, Mam—you know he won't," I insisted. "But with thirty women standing here at the gates refusing to work, he'll have to."

A murmur went through the crowd. These women were thin, tired, and poor, just like we were. Yet there was a buzz about them, an anger that gave them real dignity. When the battle began, I knew whose side I wanted to be on.

"It's not just your plight, Mary," Eliza reminded her. "We're all fed up with the long shifts and low wages—"

"And the rotten teeth!" added a woman whose face was swollen like Mam's.

"So what do we do next?" Eliza asked the group.

Someone mentioned a petition. Another woman suggested stopping work early or refusing to pay the petty fines Mr. Scott was always doling out.

"Let's make a list of what we want and

give it to Bryant," said a woman with sores on her mouth.

But I thought of what Annie had said about the promises he'd already failed to keep.

"Our best bet is to not do anything," I said. "We stay on this side of the gates and take a stand."

The women fell quiet. Thirty exhausted faces stared at me as if they hadn't quite grasped what I meant. Then the sound of a door slamming and footsteps hurrying across the yard made them turn toward the factory. Marching our way, arms swinging furiously, was Mr. Scott, the foreman.

"The shift started five minutes ago!" he

barked. "That's a late fine for all of you, and I'll be docking your pay."

No one moved.

"Did you not hear what I said?" he asked, looking genuinely bewildered.

I spoke up. "We heard you, Mr. Scott."

His gaze fell on me.

"I'm Mary Sweeney's girl," I told him, just so we were clear. "Yesterday evening you gave my mother the sack because she hadn't dipped enough matches. You knew she was ill, in awful pain because of her jaw, but you fired her anyway."

Mr. Scott laughed dryly. "Oh, bravo! A speech worthy of Mr. Dickens, I'm sure!"

"Thing is"—I moved nearer the gate—"it's not funny when a person loses their job and they can't buy food or pay their rent. It's not stuff out of a storybook, Mr. Scott. It's real life and death."

The amusement froze on his face. He stared past me, then, to the women standing behind me.

"If you want to keep your jobs, you'll be at your workbenches in two minutes," he yelled.

As he marched back into the factory, still no one moved.

"Are none of you tempted by Mr. Scott's gracious offer?" Eliza asked the group.

A couple of the women snorted in disgust.

"She's right, this one." The woman with the sore mouth nodded at me. "We need to stand firm."

Eliza agreed. "We might not have wealth or class, but we've got our dignity, and this fight is real. Enough is enough. Are we on strike?"

A cheer went up.

"Count me in, ladies. I'm with you," Mam decided.

There were more cheers, hugs for courage, then people organizing themselves into a picket line across the width of Mr. Bryant's main gates. Soon enough, we were turning delivery drivers away, stopping passersby, and singing songs to keep our spirits up and our empty stomachs off the thought of food.

In a quiet moment, Eliza said to me, "You've got a lot to say for a little match girl— a real way with words. Can you write?"

"Not yet." But I raised my chin, determined. "Though one day I will."

With such brave women beside me, anything, suddenly, felt possible. For now, though, all we wanted was a decent wage, decent working hours, and to not be poisoned. It didn't seem too much to ask.

ALMOST
A FAIRY TALE

❦

A BETTER
ENDING

THOUGH THE WORLD WASN'T quite yet ready to listen to thirty poor-as-dirt women, we certainly got people's attention. Later that first morning, on the factory side of the gates, Mr. Scott returned to threaten us, this time bringing all the other foremen with him.

"If you're not here to work, then shove off!" he bellowed. "Or I'll get the police onto you!"

"I don't think you own this sidewalk, do you, Mr. Scott?" I replied, which made the other women laugh.

The foremen glowered at us, as thick-set as bulls, but we stood our ground. With the iron bars of the gates between us, it was definitely easier to be brave. It carried on like that for an hour or more, bickering talk from both sides, but no sign of Mr. Bryant himself. When Eliza mentioned writing him a letter, I knew exactly who to ask.

*

It took me ages to find Annie's house again. But as soon as she saw me and my poor chapped feet on her doorstep, she grabbed her coat and hat and insisted on seeing the protest for herself.

Back at the factory gates, our numbers had swelled dramatically. The match workers had been joined by flower sellers, laundry workers, street sweepers, and chimney boys, the sidewalk now so full that people spilled onto the street.

"My, my," Annie murmured approvingly. "You ladies *are* causing a stir."

It was an impressive sight, I had to agree. In fact, I was bursting with pride. By mid-afternoon, the traffic had to slow to pass our protest, and the road became clogged with carts and barrows and impatient, snorting horses. Soon after that, the police arrived, just two of them, and only to get the traffic moving again.

"I probably shouldn't be saying this," one of the policemen muttered from under his hat. "But good luck to you, match girls. You deserve to be treated better."

The newspaper reporters came next. Annie seemed to know them, and they certainly knew her.

"What's your part in the story, Mrs. Besant?" they pressed her.

Annie, very politely, told them that none of this was about her. She made sure Eliza's name and Mam's appeared in their article, properly spelled and before any mention of hers.

The day ended with us tired, cold, but bolstered by one another's courage. When the bakers from Roman Road market brought us baskets of leftover bread, I burst into happy tears. This was, believe it or not, the most uplifting day I'd had in a long time.

Still, there was no sign of Mr. Bryant. But we'd be back tomorrow.

※

The protest went on for days, then weeks. It turned out Mr. Bryant only came to work on Mondays, Wednesdays, and Fridays. He'd arrive in his rust-red carriage, though we never caught sight of him, as he kept the curtains drawn when he drove through our picket line. But I like to think that he heard our jeers and shouts, or had to put his fingers in his ears to block them out.

Some days, we'd get so much support it quite choked me. Like the nuns from the local convent who made us placards out of old packing crates, painted with slogans like

SAVE OUR JOBS

and

PLEASE DON'T POISON US,

or the charity workers who brought us hot tea and buns when it rained. At times we lost heart, but mostly we could sense that, like the crocuses now emerging from the winter soil, change was on its way.

It wasn't just matches that were magic: I realized that people, working together for a purpose, could also achieve magical, magnificent things.

Annie, as I knew already, was mighty clever with a pen. Over the following months, she wrote letters and newspaper articles that gave voice to our fight in a way that made people across the entire country sit up and listen. Though her sources remained nameless in her pieces, it was obvious that she'd gotten her information from me, Mam, Eliza, and the others. She knew all the gory details—about the exhausting fourteen-hour shifts, the fines for having dirty feet or dropping matches, exactly how many workers had tooth problems (186 women, in fact). What was more, Annie knew all the foremen's names and that Mr. Scott was the worst of them. Our factory, she claimed, was a terrible, nightmarish place, not fit for animals.

So, if you're hoping for a happily ever after to my story, there is one, eventually. And it's a whole lot happier than how the famous match girl tale ends, where she dies before anyone thinks to help her. In that version, it's only the rich people who learn a moral lesson; the poor match girl ends up with nothing. She doesn't even get her slippers back.

*

The first sign that Mr. Bryant was softening was one fine spring day when he sent Mr. Scott to the factory gates with a message. The factory was offering Mam her job again. In addition, Mr. Bryant offered the rest of us an extra few pennies in our pay packets. He wouldn't budge on shortening our hours or the matter of the phosphorus, but it was a start. Despite people's kindness, those weeks without pay had taken their toll. We were all desperate to be earning again.

And so, satisfied the picket ended, the workers went back to their benches, and I returned to selling matches. For a short while after that, we had bread every day, a bit of bacon for us, and scraps for Mrs. Gladstone, the pup. When Mam bought back our candlestick from the pawnshop, she said she'd also seen a pair of boots just my size in the window and would put some money aside for them from her wages. Life was looking up.

Then Mr. Bryant received a letter from Glasgow, up in Scotland. It was an angry, attacking sort of letter, saying he should be ashamed of the dreadful conditions his workers had to endure. Red-faced with fury, Mr. Bryant marched straight to the factory floor, guessing that Mam and her colleagues were behind the message.

"How else would someone in Scotland know about us?" he demanded.

"By reading the newspapers?" Mam suggested.

"Nonsense! It's only the London papers that care to print Mrs. Besant's meddlesome rubbish."

But that wasn't the case anymore.

More newspapers across the country had taken up her articles, and so more people began to know of the match girls' plight. Farther afield, other match factories in other parts of the world had already stopped using the toxic white phosphorus.

No such luck here. Not yet.

Yet Annie's articles had shaken things up. They made Mr. Bryant nervous—so nervous that he tried to make his workers sign a petition to say they disagreed with the articles' claims. Which of course no one would, not when people's teeth were still rotting and women were fainting with illness and hunger at their benches. We needed shorter hours and safer working conditions, we told him. But Mr. Bryant wouldn't listen.

And so we went on strike again, only this time we had the whole country behind us. Yes, it meant no pay, no new boots for me, no cozy hearth or hot supper at home. But it was late spring by then, the weather warm for the time of year, and being cheered on by print workers, shopkeepers, market sellers, and road sweepers from as far afield as Liverpool and Glasgow, Truro and Cardiff, gave us a real boost. So did the food parcels that were delivered regularly by the various kind charities supporting our cause.

And if you're worried, as Mam had been, about how we'd feed an extra dog-size mouth, then all credit to Kip the slipper borrower, who now did deliveries for the butcher on Windmill Street. Twice a week, he'd bring Mrs. Gladstone a bone and scraps of meat, wrapped in newspaper. Once we'd shaken off the grease and gristle, we'd scour the paper for Mrs. Besant's articles, which Fergal would then read aloud to us. Now that the matchbox-making had stopped, he was in school every day and reading like a little scholar. I'd hear him tackle the big words without even stumbling and want to burst with pride.

※

By summer, when still no deal had been reached at the factory, we took our fight west, following the river all the way to the Houses of Parliament. The nuns made us fresh placards, and sashes to wear across our chests, and Eliza and Mam, who led the march, made up songs to sing as we walked. People lined the streets, cheering us on as if we were royalty, or soldiers coming home from war. It was the closest I'd ever felt to believing we might win.

Eventually, our voices grew so strong that Mr. Bryant had to act. The changes we'd been fighting for began to happen. Behind the factory gates, meetings were held and deals were struck. The first big change was an end to the workers' fines. Then, Mr. Scott was seen leaving the premises with a very red face, and the remaining foremen were warned that if any more bullying was reported, they'd be sacked, too.

A separate room, away from the factory floor, was set up for lunchtime. Workers could wash their hands before eating, which meant less chance of getting nasty chemicals mixed in with your bread and butter. Though it would be another decade or so before the match factory finally switched from white phosphorus to harmless red phosphorus, change had started. There was no turning back.

Finally, the factory was listening to our concerns. Wages improved more substantially, too. Mam bought me a pair of boots just in time for autumn, though by then, my brother, who'd grown upward and outward like a giant, was also in need of a new pair.

As happy endings go, ours was mostly down to a group of extraordinary women.

Though I often also wondered what part the magic played. Without those three broken matches, perhaps I'd have never truly understood why our life was so hard, that it wasn't us that was wrong, but the world we lived in, and its obsession with money.

As it was, one evening, not long after the strike ended for good, I opened a box of matches. Once upon a time, I wouldn't have dared to light a match that I could sell; it would've been a terrible waste. But now I just wanted a moment to light a match and stare into the flame. I wasn't expecting anything to happen.

Yet
as I
watched,
the flame
grew taller,
and wider,
almost too big
for such
a small,
spindly
match.

The
familiar
whooshing
feeling
came
over
me.

I was

tipping forward,

falling fast,

before landing

on a lawn on

actual, proper grass.

At the end of the

path was a little

stone cottage with

a green front door.

The door was open,

and lying there,

in a patch of

sunlight, was our

dog, older now

and snoring.

Stepping over Mrs. Gladstone, I went inside. Mam was sitting in a nice comfy chair, eating cake and drinking tea with Eliza from the factory. At the table, schoolbooks spread before him, was Fergal. Everyone looked older: Mam had gray in her hair, and Fergal a little shadow over his top lip. Seeing me come in, he handed me a book, which I supposed meant this was our future and I'd learned to read and write at last.

"You're a better storyteller than this chap, Bridie," he claimed. "I'd much rather read your version of being a match girl."

I turned the spine toward me and, seeing the name of the book, smiled. He was right, my brother. In my *Little Match Girl* story, there was a hopeful ending, and it didn't involve anyone dying in the snow. Taking Fergal's advice, I pulled up a chair beside him and began to write everything down.

A NOTE FROM
THE AUTHOR

The original Little Match Girl story was published in 1845 and is often described as a fairy tale, though the ending isn't a happy one. *In Victorian times, sad, sentimental stories were popular, but it didn't seem fair to me that the match girl dies in the end. So I decided to write my own version, where she has a name, a loving family, and her own hopes and dreams.*

Bridie Sweeney's story begins on New Year's Eve, 1887. In Victorian London at this time, there would have been thousands of children like her, earning a meager living selling matches, shoelaces, and newspapers on the city streets. Despite a law stating that children up to the age of twelve now had to go to school, many of the poorest families needed the children's earnings and sent them out to work.

When she's thirteen, Bridie will be old enough to work inside the match factory with her mother. True accounts tell us of terrible conditions on the factory floor. The workers did fourteen-hour shifts, with only two short breaks, and had to eat their meals at their workbenches. They were in daily contact with a highly toxic substance called white phosphorus. It caused many health problems: headaches, tiredness, and an extremely painful type of bone disease known as "phossy jaw."

My story takes place in and around the real Bryant & May match factory, in Bow, in the East End of London. The factory employed thousands of women and girls from the local area, where some of the poorest families in the city lived. Despite the company's huge profits, workers were poorly paid and management did little to recognize the health risks they faced.

In 1888, a woman was wrongly dismissed from her job, and the other factory workers went on strike. This caught the attention of Annie Besant, a political activist who spoke out against poverty and in favor of rights for women.

Her letters, published in national news-papers, made people across the country aware of the terrible conditions in which the factory staff worked and lived. The strike attracted huge levels of public support: charities were set up, donations made, and everywhere they went, the strikers were met with cheers. That summer, the women marched all the way to Parliament with their cause.

Eventually, worried for their reputation, the factory owners agreed to their workers' demands. Pay and conditions were improved, but it wasn't until 1908 that the use of white phosphorus was finally banned. The strike was, and still is, one of the most impressive accounts of a workforce standing up for their right to fair treatment. This, I believe, is the ending all match girls deserve.

Emma Carroll, Somerset, England, 2022

A NOTE FROM
THE ILLUSTRATOR

This story beautifully merges fairy tale with fact, delivering a piece of history that has real resonance for us today. It was such a pleasure to research the illustrations for Bridie's story, and I was fortunate to find a great many photographs relating to the living conditions of the factory workers. The characters I have drawn are based on historical photographs, too, adapted of course, but reflecting their expressions and body language,

combined with Emma's descriptions.

The clothing, hairstyles, and fashions of the time are taken from these pictures, though there is a bit of artistic license when it comes to the patterns and textures used. The paintwork of the houses and the decoration of the Christmas tree are also taken from historical sources. The matches of the day didn't have red tips, but it seemed like a nice motif to use in the book, reflecting Bridie's flame-red hair and the defiance of the strikers.

Lauren Child, London, 2022